D0705994

RADIO CACOPHONY

Radio Cacophony

Published by Big Lucks Books
Austin, TX
BigLucks.com

ISBN: 978-1-941985-06-9

Cover design by Sally Anne Morgan
Book design by Mark Cugini

Titles set in Avant Garde LT
Text set in Crimson

First edition, September 2016

radio cacophony

michelle dove

BIG LUCKS BOOKS 2016

for Elliott

*

The deejay on-air is sobbing. Or is it: The deejay is sobbing on-air? As we argue which of the sentences is more correct, we forget entirely that there is clearly something wrong with the deejay. Only when the lights go dim in the studio and the airwaves go dead do we venture down the hallway to check in on the deejay. Is there a deejay in here who can use a good shoulder to cry on? Or, perhaps: Can the deejay who's in here use a good cry on a shoulder? When the deejay stops crying because she is now more perplexed at our questions than she is upset about her own problems, only then do we see the true value in semantics.

*

The Public Relations Manager is in charge of updating the PSAs on the PSA ring. The Production Manager is in charge of updating the PSAs on the minidisc. At first I only play the prerecorded PSAs at the designated Public Service Announcement times, quarter-past and quarter-till. When I start hating the sound of my own voice less, I sometimes read the PSAs off the PSA ring. It's only then evident to me that the PSAs on the PSA ring and the PSAs on the minidisc are identical, meaning that it makes no difference to the listener whether or not I play the prerecorded PSAs or voice the PSAs myself. The same is true of the station identification—it doesn't matter if at the top of the hour and the bottom of the hour I play the prerecorded station identification or if I voice it, since they accomplish the exact same thing. Eventually I believe other things in my life will make just as much sense.

*

The studio is down the hall from the office. The stereo in the office always plays what the studio's broadcasting over the airwaves. As the Office Manager I have been issued an official key to the office, which means I don't have to persuade the custodial staff to let me in. I convince people that I come to the office to work. I am not upset with the public face of this lie, as I am privately pleased that I have nowhere else to go. Sometimes I sleep between classes on the donated leather couch. The Librarian calls the donated leather couch the conjugal couch when we get high in the stacks. The Librarian says he's lost count of how many times someone's had sex on this couch. Days later when I wake from a long nap, I'm unsure if I dreamed about a nautical carnival tour because of the gypsy punk playing over the airwaves as I slept or because of what I can't unknow about the couch.

*

I read somewhere that girls everywhere are getting pregnant and dropping out of college. I refuse to be a statistic, so I keep a complimentary Health Center condom in my backpack at all times. But I worry that in the confines of the backpack the condoms expire before I can ever use them. Over time I become too disheartened to keep throwing out the old condom and replacing it with a new condom. What a hassle! Eventually I stop going to the Health Center altogether, even for annual checkups, having irrationally convinced myself that preparing for sex I'll never have is worse than having a child I never wanted.

*

Today's theme on the Mystery Secret Theme Show is a still mystery. Ninety minutes in and do we have a clue? No, we have no clue! Maybe the deejay will be nice enough this time to give us a handout. We listen intently every time he comes on the mic to announce the last few tracks that came to us initially unannounced: Lee Morgan, Herbie Nichols, Captain Beefheart, Cap'n Jazz, Frank London's Klezmer Brass Allstars. But what do these names have in common? The show is almost over and still we have no clue. We can only walk to the bar shaking our heads and asking ourselves, What was it even all about? Do you think we'll ever know what it was all about?

*

In the student commons I find them where they said they'd be and by what description, only they're less my equal in age than I'd hoped. The balding one with maybe the word H-E-A-T or H-E-A-P tattooed across his knuckles asks me why I applied to be Music Director. He doesn't take the toothpick out of his mouth before asking, indicating that he either just ate a big meal or is plagued with an oral fixation worse than the one that plagues me. I name what I will later learn are irrelevant hardcore and metal bands, names I only know thanks to my skater boyfriend from high school. Do they know I can differentiate among these bands about as well as I can guess my present company's ages? The General Manager, who is the bearded one and maybe thirty, calls me three days later. He presents me with a choice: Office Manager or Public Relations Manager. I am technically majoring in communication but don't know what exactly constitutes public relations. I say Office Manager and hang up and tell my roommate, who is for now still my roommate and technically the only person I have to tell these things, that something great has happened: I'm now part of something I know nothing about.

*

One afternoon a butterfly makes its way into the studio and lands on the deejay's shoulder. The deejay gets on-air to announce his good fortune. As My Bloody Valentine's "Blown a Wish" plays over the airwaves, we all gather in the studio and proceed with a spontaneous blessing ritual. The deejay then cups the butterfly gently in his hands and releases it through the studio window to freedom. Weeks later a bumblebee makes its way into the studio. The deejay shrieks and we come rushing down the hall to see her stricken in the studio corner. We try coaxing the bumblebee through the open window but it swarms about erratically before landing on the turntable mere feet from the stricken deejay. As we wait to see who among us will be brave enough to approach the bumblebee in its vulnerable state, the deejay pulls the record closest to her from its sleeve and in a hasty motion smashes the bumblebee on the turntable. We are horrified. Only we are not entirely sure if the death of the bumblebee causes us more grief than the biotic smear that has irrefutably formed underneath the record.

*

When Fun Pauly gets to my Radiothon theme, he doesn't read the description that explains that my show is in tandem with Keely's show. He thinks I have copied Keely. He says I have to get a new theme because I can't do the same theme as Keely. I wait for Keely to explain that we're doing a theme in tandem but she's having maybe a thumb war with the Promotions Director and doesn't look up or say anything. I stop taking the minutes when Fun Pauly moves on to the next theme. I can't not sit there trying to think up a new theme. I know that the themes one can choose from or make up are infinite. Despite knowing this, I can't think of a theme that's not already been picked.

*

Initially, the bonfire doesn't draw the authority's attention. Nobody stops the frat boys next door from bringing their own cups and pouring themselves beer from the keg. Later in the night when the frat boys carry over the couch they vow to burn, I tell Keely maybe we should leave. I watch the couch burn so intently that I forget to follow Keely inside when she finally heads into the house. On one side of me in the backyard are the jazz deejays and the husky-yet-sexy girl who fronts the local punk outfit Mostly Forever. On the other side are the drunk frat boys. I don't know if I have a choice between which side to pick, or if since nobody's talking to me there's really nothing I get to decide. I'd been told that there are fewer mosquitoes around when there's fire or smoke but when my knuckles start to swell and itch I realize this isn't scientific. When the cops appear moments later and I'm cited for underage possession of alcohol, I cannot stop scratching my knuckles. Despite the despair I will surely feel in the morning, the involuntary motion brings me comfort. And comfort is only so far off from control.

*

Is there more to the Smiths than we think? Clearly there's more to the Smiths than we think, but to find out, we'd have to actually listen to the Smiths' albums, over and over and over, until eventually we aren't saying, Is this the song that we like? but are instead saying, Oh, this is the song that we like. Which is really the prelude, we all know, to simply liking all the songs that the Smiths sing. Because once the songs seep in as if a part of us, there's no turning back, no way to unlike the Smiths once our inner ears and, let's face it, our hearts have committed to liking them. And if we've learned anything from listening or not listening to the bands that we aren't sure what we really think about, it's precisely that: there's more to anything than we think.

*

Keely says it's all guesswork but I've been in the studio before when the Chief Engineer plays Radio Cacophony. Layering one record over another over another over another is more than guesswork, I say. It's an art. The Chief Engineer is the first to admit that the layering can be unnerving and sometimes sound just plain wrong. But the art is in the melding of ambience with amperage and energies and vocals. The art is the recognition that just because something already is recorded and fixed one way that it doesn't mean it can't be played back another way. I try to explain this to Keely the night she comes over to hang out in my dorm when my roommate is out. Keely listens to what I'm saying and what the Chief Engineer is doing on the radio but is distracted constantly by the accessories in my roommate's closet. Do you think she'll notice if I take one of these belts? Keely asks. She asks, Don't you think I'd look good in this belt?

*

I keep my hands in my pockets because they're shaking. I ask the notorious hip-hop deejay if he knows what's in the package and why it's addressed to him. The notorious hip-hop deejay says the busted ink cartridges are a joke, that his buddy in LA works at an office supply chain and likes to mess with him. I ask if he thinks I was born yesterday. I ask if there are what I think there are underneath all the busted ink cartridges. The notorious hip-hop deejay says, No! Of course not! I ask what I should do with the box of busted ink cartridges. He says, Don't worry! I'll toss it for you! My hands are shaking less because when he picks up the box I know he's about to leave. I say, No more packages better show up with your name on them. I say, You're not even on staff. I say, You could get us all arrested. To this day I don't know if my accusation was valid or not, but I do know what it feels like to confront someone who I suspect of running a racket.

*

We give away four of the promotional festival tickets but keep the other four to dole out to the staff. We draw four names from the hat, but once someone realizes that the four names we drew aren't present, this someone suggests that these are the four people who aren't getting the promotional tickets. We draw three more names of those who aren't getting the tickets and the remaining four names get the tickets: John (General Manager), Gus (Promotions Director), Fun Pauly (Music Director) and Keely (Public Relations Manager). I don't record the names of the four people getting the tickets in the minutes because I am in that moment told not to, since for all intents and purposes, and if the faculty advisor asks, we gave these promotional festival tickets to the third caller to Kevin-and-Kevin's morning show.

*

I choose "Bands with Animals in Them." I want to make the title catchy so I change it to "Banimals: Bands with Animals in Them." The Librarian catches me taking CDs from the stacks and ripping copies on the office computer. He says ripping copies the way I might say sleeping sideways, all lava-like and overenunciated. He asks if I want to get high in the stacks and I'm not uncertain he isn't blackmailing me. I walk to the dorms that afternoon the long way, knowing when I see my roommate she'll want to know why I smoked up without her. I plan to play her the new CDs I ripped whether she's interested in hearing new bands or not or whether I think they're good or not, since clearly I don't trust my own taste in music anymore. I plan to invite her to the station's next keg party whether she wants to go or not. I count myself lucky when I return to the dorm and she's not there and I'm still high enough to enjoy what music I technically just stole in solitude.

*

Technically speaking, they say, they are not emo. They are not post-punk revival. They are not dream pop. They are, they say, something of a hybrid. Can we not see how their eclectic sound defies genre? We can see how their eclectic sound defies genre, we say, although we do not entirely mean it. They have a repertoire of nine songs, which they play in the same strict order when they open for bands touring through our town. We tire of these nine songs but have no other hometown band to support. We have restless fandom energies that need to be directed somewhere. When we get drunk with the band after a good set, we try to push them down a pigeonhole. Who are your current influences? we ask. Who do you think sounds most like you? Wouldn't you say you're categorically more no wave than classic noise? But they see right through our tricks. No matter how many shots of tequila we buy them, they do not give us the satisfaction we seek. Years later the band makes a record that garners buzz throughout college radio. They distribute promotional photos and issue press releases. They are featured in a prominent music magazine, where a journalist cites them as a neo-shoegaze band to look out for. Ah-ha! we want to say to them. There! But they moved out of town years ago and we do not know their address or phone number. According to their band bio they are living somewhere in Brooklyn.

*

Halfway through the semester I am told that everything about the radio station is said to be the most fun ever. Someone coins the phrase "Funnest Radio Station in the World" and once one deejay says it on-air, then another, and another, it's like an echo in a cave that never stops. The Promotions Director takes the liberty to put "Funnest Radio Station in the World" on the new promotional T-shirts, mugs, stickers, and buttons. Eventually at a staff meeting when someone points out that the word funnest makes us look brainless and maybe even the opposite of actual fun, someone wants to know who coined the phrase. The Business Manager says the Librarian did. The Librarian says the Junior Sales Manager did. The Junior Sales Manager says I did. Nobody can remember who said it first. Nobody admits saying it first. I act like I'm documenting the discussion in the meeting minutes but when I type them later that week I leave out the origin of funnest conversation entirely. I am unsure what to do when there's no resolution in these meetings, which is often the case. I am unsure that I'm not invisible even amidst the strong personalities all around me.

*

My roommate says on the one hand she really does want to like riot grrrl bands but, on the other hand, she doesn't want to seem too feminist and inadvertently give the boys she meets the wrong idea. I put five canonical riot grrrl bands in the CD changer and hit random. We pour ourselves vodka oranges because even in our second semester of college it's the classiest mixed drink we dare to make. After five minutes it's clear she cannot lie on her bunk and stare at the ceiling and just listen. She says she met a boy in her chemistry intro who's pledging Delta Upsilon. She says he asked her what her favorite type of food is and she said Italian, what her favorite band is and she said duh, Dave Matthews, hands down, what her favorite type of liquor is and she said vodka. She's still talking when I finally understand the difference between Bikini Kill and Huggy Bear. When my roommate gets dressed to meet the boy in her chemistry intro at the dining hall, I turn up the volume to an ungodly level. I can see in the mirror that she looks disgusted. When she returns after midnight, visibly smitten with new love, I am drunk enough to admit that I listened to the records three times each. Yet I am sober enough to know that I am the epitome of pointless liars, and by three I really mean four.

*

Whoever's name we draw out of the hat has to take the first shift at the poster sale. I'm in favor of not drawing names out of a hat but in nominating the Junior Sales Manager to go first. Reluctantly I mix up the names in the hat and let Fun Pauly draw one out. When he chooses his own name his face goes slack and he says he was never in favor of a poster sale to raise money anyhow, since what do mass produced posters of nineteenth century paintings have to do with post-rock or indie rock or punk rock, let alone hip-hop or new wave or bluegrass? We take a vote of all those in favor or not in favor of the poster sale. But when the tally is in the Business Manager says we cannot vote down the poster sale because we won't have money to pay for the promotional T-shirts, mugs, stickers, and buttons we've already ordered. To weight his argument, the Business Manager volunteers to take the first shift at the poster sale. But do any of us immediately volunteer to take the second shift at the poster sale? Do any of us follow his selfless lead? Secretly, I am glad. I wish failure on no one, but I've always hoped to witness a martyr waste his zeal on an ignoble cause.

*

The one I like plays a Day Art show of classic and new indie pop. The one who likes me plays electronica on Saturday nights. The one Keely likes does a blues show on Friday afternoons. The one the blues deejay likes doesn't work at the radio station at all—she's just a bashful girl from the newspaper across the hall. The trick is to never show up to the studio during the show of a deejay who you don't like or of a deejay whose music you don't like because you might cast a false impression of how you feel about them or their music. Sometimes you can call to request a song from a deejay whose music you don't like to more or less trick them to play better music, and sometimes if you mask your voice with a certain tone they may not think your calling has anything to do with how you feel about them. The last week of the semester I show up during the Day Art show of the one I like, only to find Keely there updating the PSA ring. And since I don't know if she's there to update the PSA ring or because she now likes the Day Art deejay who I like, I err on the side of least embarrassment and check to see what new music came in the mail and leave.

*

My roommate is lying on her bunk and I am lying on my bunk. When the phone rings, my roommate says, You get it, since it's probably for me. I answer, and my roommate props herself on her elbows to watch the one-sided exchange. I nod as the boy on the other end explains where he'd like to take me Friday night, what he'd like to show me, what he'd like to buy me, et cetera, but what I want to say is, This is some kind of mistake, hold on, you must've confused us, let me put my roommate on. After he finishes with his pitch, I'm dumbfounded. My roommate is staring at the ceiling again, huffing through her dragon lungs. I say the only thing I can, which is to the effect of, I'm sorry, but I have plans on Friday. I thank him for calling and hang up. Still dumbfounded, I climb back onto my bunk and stare at the ceiling alongside my roommate. When the phone rings again, neither of us move to answer it. It keeps ringing, so finally I do what has to be done. Hello? I say. The boy on the other end must know he doesn't need to apologize to me. So he doesn't. He only says, Oh hey, is your roommate around? So I pass the phone to her and she smiles.

*

A boy in my Shakespeare seminar walks me to my dorm after class. After he walks me to my dorm two weeks straight I invite him in to see my dorm room. The very first time we are alone we fool around. Weeks pass. He walks me to my dorm after every class, and I continue to invite him inside. Soon I cannot read Shakespeare without thinking of his hands on my breasts. One Friday I hear someone in class tell him they're excited for the party later. What party's that? I ask when his mouth is hovering over my nipple. Only then does he invite me, claiming that it won't be that much fun. I've always wanted to see his bedroom, only I had imagined it wouldn't be against the backdrop of a drunken ruckus. When I see him in class on Monday and he doesn't ask why I didn't show to the party, my self-respect skyrockets. I sneak out of class early, taking a shortcut to my dorm, my body exhilarated by what I've done. It takes months to undo the damage, but one day by the campus pond I feel release! I close the anthology and skip all the way home, warmed and carefree that Ophelia's death no longer arouses me.

*

Once the News Director discovers my obsession with Philly cheesesteaks, it's us at the grocery store getting the necessary ingredients and beer. Once we're back at his apartment, it's him prepping the peppers and onions and condiments while I choose a record to put on the stereo. Once a record's on the stereo and the steak's frying in the pan, it's him telling me how really he's a good dancer, promise! Then it's him showing me how good of dancer he is, twirling me like a melting snow cone round and round the room. Once the cheesesteaks are ready, it's him telling me that these don't look like the best he's ever made so don't judge so readily, OK? Then it's the cheesesteak in my mouth and me thinking the cheese is so gross and gooey but I wash it down with the beer and let nothing out of my mouth but praise. Hours later, it's me thinking that it is beer—not cheese—that is truly gross and gooey. Until before long it's only my body spread across the couch, and me mumbling about how much I like Sonic Youth after all—they're not so inaccessible. Their lyrics are just sort of dumb, is all.

*

When I dial the number my hands are shaking. She answers like anyone who isn't famous would—Hello? And I am calm enough to say the same—Hello? But then the harder part kicks in, and I must introduce myself in the official capacity I hold and begin asking the questions I'd prepared. What other bands or female artists inspire your music? Do you play any other instruments besides guitar? Were you a nervous child that took to music to combat your neuroses? Did it work? If you had any advice for aspiring musicians today, would that advice double as song lyrics? Would it be safe to say that you're writing new lyrics in your head as we speak? She answers each question with an answer that seems less and less polished, only as her answers become less and less polished my questions become more and more rigid. As if we are the inverse of the other. I laugh nervously as I make this discovery and she laughs nervously too, not because I think she's thinking that we are the inverse of each other by any means, but because her newborn begins crying in the background and she has to bring the crying child closer to the phone to apply motherly comfort. What was I saying? she says at that point. And because my hands are still shaking, I wasn't taking notes. And because I knew I could listen to her answer again on the recording playback, I also wasn't taking notes. I do not know what to say. I do not know what she was saying. And when I simply ask the question I had already asked a second time, she doesn't say, Oh, right. What I was saying was . . . like I hope she'll say. Instead she says, I think I answered that one already. And I say, Oh right. And she says, Well, it's been nice talking to you. And I say, It sure has. I'm a huge fan. And she says, Goodbye now. And it's only after I

hang up that I realize that if the crying child wasn't crying I may have remembered to ask her to voice a station identification. I think then that maybe I should call her back and ask her to voice the station identification after all. But then I think again of the crying baby and the questions I asked and the shaking in my hands and before I lock up the production booth I do what I must and press a series of buttons which erases the interview completely.

*

At the local coffee shop I am greeted by another deejay studying in a booth by the window. I apologize for cutting the conversation short, explaining how I'm supposed to be on-air in ten minutes. Will he be listening to the show? He will be listening to the show, he says. Of course! Will he call in a request if the moment strikes him? Yes, he will call in a request if the moment strikes him. I continue my stroll to the station, equally pleased with the latte I am drinking and the knowledge that one of my comrades will be listening to the show. I play an eclectic set, hoping it will inspire a range of possible songs that my comrade can request. I anticipate his call the entire show. When I'm down to the last fifteen minutes, I dedicate a song to him, hoping then he will call in with his most anticipated request. Walking home after the show, I am distraught to have never heard from my comrade. Days later I run into him in the coffee shop again and we talk lengthily about the coffee shop's great coffee and scones. Neither of us brings up the show. To this day I am unsure if he didn't listen to the show like he said he would or if he did listen and was appalled by the music I played. Further, I am unsure which of these scenarios, if true, would damage me more.

*

Why do we hate his radio show? We can admit we're not connoisseurs of house music. We clearly don't have the talent or stamina to count beats the same way, even for Radio Cacophony. But we have taste, right? And the way he bobs his head when he walks! And those stupid white tennis shoes he's always wearing. And the sound of his voice in a room, all like, Hey guys, who wants to get high before the show? Ha ha ha—not with you, buddy, am I right? It isn't our fault that he's standing there, just then, in the shadows, hearing us talk. How hard is it to play it off like we were talking about someone else? And when he transfers schools at the end of the semester and comes by the station to let us know that we were the only real friends he had at school, we feel like assholes. Assholes with better taste than him, it's true, but of course we know even this means we're still assholes.

*

The one my roommate wants has wall-to-wall carpet and central air and an in-unit washer/dryer stack and is within spitting distance of frat row. The one I want has hardwood floors that warble a little when you walk over them at any gait and a back patio that butts up against some community gardens that you can walk through to get downtown faster. It's one month till the dorms close for summer so we have to make a decision fast. We do rock, paper, scissors, but when I win my roommate says it's unfair, she wasn't ready. So we do rock, paper, scissors again and she wins, but instead of saying, OK, we'll live in the one you want, I say, You know what? Fuck this. My roommate is so appalled at my reaction she storms into the courtyard barefoot and guileless. For the next hour I hear her cry, telling everyone who stops to comfort her what a bitch I am. Hearing her distress, I know I will later feel terrible for abandoning my roommate. But what I know even more in this moment is something even more terrible to admit—I don't yet know enough about myself to compromise.

*

The balding one with maybe the word H-E-A-T or H-E-A-P tattooed on his knuckles will never get close enough to me so I can verify what word is on his knuckles. Only when I get into the cellar bar underage and drink three vodka cranberries, which I immediately discover are way better than vodka oranges, do I get close enough to him to see that the word is H-E-A-T. Only when I get drunk and close enough to him does the balding one put his arm around my shoulder to steady me as I walk home, and only when we get there do I realize it's not my home but his home. And when I wake up the next morning only to find my clothes in different pockets across the floor, it's only then that I realize I was so drunk that I was mistaken. The word is definitely H-E-A-P.

*

Keely agrees to buy the grill for our patio if I buy the charcoal for the whole summer. We send emails to the staff that say, The fire's hot—bring your own burger! When we run out of lime wedges, I cut more lime wedges for the beers the neighbors bought us, and Keely puts on records when the deejay plays more than two songs in a row we don't like. Only when the Librarian and the Promotions Director are still there as the sun is rising does Keely forget about all our teamwork and get up abruptly and go to bed. I watch the sunrise waiting to see if it's the Librarian or the Promotions Director who wanders inside first, but before I can find out who's crushing harder on Keely, I'm so drunk and tired I fall asleep slouched in the patio chair. When I wake up midday the radio isn't even on. No one is outside on the patio or in the apartment with me, not even Keely.

*

We choose "Is Hip-hop Literature? A Dissertation" because we think we can stretch the theme the full five hours, even if no one calls in a request. With two more hours to go the delusions begin, and there I am saying, I'm sorry, it's all my fault, I'm too eager to set examples. And the Production Manager saying, It's OK, I don't blame you, I was trying to prove Gus wrong, is all. And my eyelids drooping farther down, and me saying, Wait, what? What's to prove? And the Production Manager sitting next to me on the couch when the record starts to skip, and us not caring one flying elephant's bone, and him saying, Well, Gus and I bet on who would sleep with you first. And me saying, What? You made a bet? And me falling asleep for a split second, and then waking, as if in a different body that's now speaking for itself, For how much? And us making out for a minute on the couch, then in the stacks, the Production Manager's hands running over parts of me that have atrophied in sleep, until the phone finally rings, and the caller yelling, I'll pledge five dollars to make this reeking skipping stop! And us shouting, Hallelujah! We won't come up empty after all! And us looking at each other in that moment, unsure where to put our hands or our mouths at all anymore, but it doesn't matter, does it, because we know what's important, which is us now aroused enough to make it to the shift change at 7 AM.

*

The Night Art deejay stands there in disbelief, counting aloud the number of records I've let pile up next to the console. Twenty-seven records! he exclaims. And I would've started putting away the ones I'd played and maybe even a few I hadn't played right then if I wasn't wondering why the Night Art deejay showed up to my Day Art show in the first place. He keeps standing there too, looking at the announcements for shows taped on the bulletin board, which is really just a painted red wall with no art on it, so isn't it screaming for someone to flyer it? If I didn't know any better, I'd think you were about to try out some Radio Cacophony, he says. And for a brief second I think that if he wasn't there and wasn't making me more nervous than usual I'd consider playing at least two records at once, to see at the very least how two things at once feels.

*

One of the twins visits me during my Day Art show, only I am not immediately sure which of the twins he is. To hide my embarrassment, I ask a series of questions to decipher whether he is Twin A or Twin B. How are classes going? Are you enjoying your radio show? Wasn't that you I saw in a back booth at the bar the other night? To my dismay, his answers do not definitely prove if he is Twin A or Twin B. In my frantic effort to unearth his identity, I suddenly remember that Twin A has a more polished radio voice. Immediately I put him to the test. I cue the mics. I introduce a surprise guest and nod to him, hoping he will speak up. But before he has a chance to say anything of substance, several things occur that demand my immediate attention. The record in the background starts skipping. The mics elicit shrieks of feedback. The record I reach to put on next is missing from the record sleeve. In the commotion, I fail to decipher who this person visiting my show is after all. Years later, I often see Twin B, who lives across the city, and, on occasion, Twin A, who often comes to the city to visit Twin B. Their features and personalities are so striking and disparate that I cannot imagine what had ever caused me to construe them as one.

*

The music on the AM frequency is more enjoyable today than the music on the FM frequency. But the dial in the station's office is always tuned to the FM frequency, since the AM frequency is more for deejays to practice being deejays. To listen to the music on the AM frequency, we thus must mute the stereo in the station office entirely, something which is practically unprecedented, and kindly ask the AM deejays if they wouldn't mind turning their music up a bit. Of course the AM deejays smile at this, since they're not even real deejays yet, only apprentices, and happily turn up the volume in the AM studio. But before too long the FM deejay is in the hallway, rapping on the window to the AM studio, saying, Hey, turn that down in there! Can't hear my own thoughts! And the AM deejays are shouting back, The staff asked us to turn it up, doofus! Ask them! And eventually the FM deejay ponders this long enough and comes into the office, all frantic-like, saying, What gives, guys! Did you tell those little tasteless morons to turn up the volume? But we pretend that we don't hear the frantic nature in the FM deejay's voice. We only turn up the volume on the stereo, which is now back on, playing the FM frequency, and say, Shhh, this is a great song, right? We just love this song. And the FM deejay stands there for a moment before realizing that it's his show we're listening to and says, Yeah? Me too!

*

The Night Art deejay visits my show only one other time, yet the time is a memorable time. We talk for hours. We laugh without restraint. When I complain of the kink in my neck, he gives me an impromptu backrub. His hands relax me on-air in a way I've never been relaxed before. Although he never returns to see me, I come to desire the relaxation of the backrub every time I go on-air. Weeks later I tune into his show, hoping that the sound of his voice will relax me as his hands once did. It doesn't, and eventually the sound of his voice causes me so much stress that I furtively hope he never visits my show again.

*

The TV cameras and marching band's parade through campus signal that the championship game is upon us. The streets overflow with apparel. The bars fill with jerseys. Fearing what harm we may inflict on strangers, Fun Pauly leads an impromptu retreat to the studio. We huddle together for warmth, wondering if this isn't the best place to ride out the apocalypse too. We pass out graham crackers and marshmallows and squares of chocolate. The News Director uses his lighter for the first round. The chocolate squares melt even as the marshmallows remain unchanged. We play angry music and impersonate jocks on-air. Most of us drink so heavily we provisionally forget the name of our own school's mascot. Years later a slew of former deejays invite me to their tailgate at a National Football League game. I feel ashamed at first that we are now a part of the same mass who delights in sports events. Then Fun Pauly appears in an oversized jersey, driving what appears to be a motorized drink cooler full of vodka and Red Bulls. At the sight of him the shame I feel for everyone quickly vanishes, leaving only humiliation enough for one.

*

After many drinks the Librarian confesses that the other guy had more experience than me. He says, He's a business major, for chrissake! On the one hand, I'm elated. I was always decent at algebra. On the other hand, I'm nervous. I don't know the first thing about business, let alone managing. The bartender is a fan of the radio station even though he absolutely, one-hundred percent hates Kevin-and-Kevin's morning show. He pours us a round of shots. To the blues! we all shout. To the blues! It's only then when I notice my freshman roommate drinking what looks like vodka cranberries in a back booth with her new boyfriend. Impulsively, I take my shot and when the bartender's pouring another round I leave through the side door before I or my old roommate can infect each other's new lives in ways we may or may not later regret. Days later when I run into my old roommate across the student commons, I realize our meeting again is inevitable. And don't I want to be the bigger person? I call out her name and wave, but when she doesn't immediately turn around, I instinctively crouch down and lower my head and pretend I am just some anonymous person stopping to tie her shoe.

*

One night when Keely is out, I accept an invitation to drink rum punch with the neighbors. There are three boys in total and none of them are unattractive. Late into the night I lie in the wet grass and gaze up at the stars, feeling as if I will never tire of their attention. I wake the next day in an unfamiliar bedroom. I quietly return to my apartment next door, overjoyed to have inaugurated what could be a casual and continuous sexual exchange. Days later I wake in the same unfamiliar bedroom. But then it is weeks before the neighbors wave me over through the window again. The neighbor who has claimed me waits until we are almost in his bedroom before confessing that he's getting back together with his ex-girlfriend. I'm so intoxicated I become hysterical. That's great! I say. Terrific! I'm too drunk to realize that my happiness for him in this moment isn't real. But equally upsetting is my undeniably selfish wish that I had liaised with a different neighbor from the start.

*

No one has a better idea or place to be at 4 AM so I lead the way. In less than ten minutes, we move the conjugal couch out of the office and into the studio, while simultaneously moving the studio couch out of the studio and into the office. Although technically we are unsure if the conjugal couch has known more sexual feats over time than the studio couch, we vow not to invert the names of the couches. Weeks later when I stop by the station between classes, I find the couches have been swapped back. In my panic that we have been found out, I accuse everyone. I post flyers and send out emails that read: Who did this? Did you do this? At first I believe it could have only been a staff member who had a key to the office. But what if it was someone who persuaded the custodial staff to let them in? When no one confesses, we live with the new former arrangement from then on, only with the knowledge that the couches weren't always located where they are located. Try as we might, we cannot unknow the history of where the couches have been.

*

Is it because as a child I was never introduced to pop music? Is it because I was never encouraged to explore any breadth of sound? Is it because I quit piano lessons when I was eleven, because against my parents' instructions I listened to secular radio in my headphones as I fell asleep? Is it because I quit the basketball team to get stoned with my skater boyfriend instead? Because I watched his horrendous band practice in basements and garages and compose one terribly pointless song after another? Is it because I was conditioned that pop music is satanic? Is it because it is in my nature to rebel and thus I fell deep into an abyss of sound hoping that my soul was at stake in the pit of it? In the extreme desire for understanding, I am all too aware that the questionnaire I give myself is impractical. Method is always circumspect. The blue jeans I'm wearing are outdated. The coffee tastes better in the ceramic mug. And the answers that I tell myself—they are but one truth.

*

When we play the Julie Ruin song that curses in many places we must mute out the many curses for fear of being reprimanded. And isn't it somebody who is maybe-not-up-for-it always having to set an example? But later that week a deejay plays a curse-filled track and fails to mute any of the curses. And later still another deejay curses on-air because maybe his girlfriend broke up with him unexpectedly and maybe he is drunk before noon and maybe he should have found a sub but didn't and now the mic is on and it is too late to stop him from embarrassing himself. So it is the cursing that is adding up and it is our fear that is increasing and it is our minds worrying about how poorly we are managing the radio station after all. But weeks later when no FCC or campus police or authority figures show to chastise us it is none of these things. It is only us returning to our Day Art show and cueing the mics without any tenderness or fragility. Only us playing a string of grooveless and cacophonous sounds, wondering if anyone is even listening at all.

*

Only when driving across Colorado years later do I come across what can only be a college radio station. As the deejay plays '90s-era post rock, I recall bands I haven't thought about in years. Only then am I reminded of the staying power of these bands and wonder why I haven't played these bands on long drives before. Slint! Moonshake! Gastr del Sol! And what of the band with the prominent theremin? Who's the band with the prominent theremin again? When the deejay comes on-air to list the tracks he's played, only then do I turn up the car stereo to find out the name of the mystery band. Only when after several minutes I fail to hear the names of any bands at all do I realize the deejay's recounting his late night at his friend's backyard bonfire. When he continues to ramble on about his previous whereabouts, only then do I become enraged. I want to blame the deejay for my frustration, only I know it's the fault of my own failing memory that I will spend the rest of the drive tormented by the name of the band I can't remember.

*

Keely and I choose "Boy on Girl/Girl on Boy," meaning every song has both male and female vocals. We do not drink as heavily as usual the night before, meaning our delivery is likely off. But still we make a killing! Only we don't know if the reason for the pledges to our show is because 1) we have actual fans or 2) because we are the only current show hosted by two females. We are not so naive to admit that the latter might be truer, although we do not have any evidence that it's not the former either. We weigh the pros and cons of it being the latter first, thinking that it would be flattering to know that guys were interested in dating us because if we are this witty and fun on the radio, wouldn't we be more so in person? Only then do we weigh the pros and cons of the former, realizing it would be even more flattering to know that people out there appreciated the music we played so much that it impacted their lives in positive ways and really got them thinking. Only then does the phone ring, and we think, Goody, another donation! The caller is not calling to donate, however, since the caller is my skater boyfriend from high school. When I ask him what he wants, fearing the worst of all possible wants, he's silent. Finally he says, I just wanted to confirm it is really you who likes all this strange music now. Eventually after a small eternity of silence I get off the phone with him and ask Keely, What were we talking about again? Only then does the conversation reach a higher level and we realize that the latter would be the worst possible scenario, since that would mean callers are more or less donating money to get in our pants. And if they ever did get in our pants, whether by accident or by choice, what would that by defacto make us?

*

The moment we realize we haven't watched TV in weeks and we feel something like whole or pure is the same moment some asshole plays that sappy Lifehouse song on-air and we're like, Are you kidding me! Isn't this the jazz hour? So instead of marching in the studio, the General Manager is all refined, calling up the deejay, May we have a word, sir? So here the asshole comes, not looking sheepish or regretful at all, which is why the General Manager says, I should demote you to AM sooo fast...To which I think, Yes, let 'em have it, we've got you now, buddy! To which my surprise follows when the asshole says in his own defense, But I played it for my girlfriend! It's our anniversary! It's her favorite! And what we want to say then is how hard his girlfriend must suck, can't he see? But we know that even if she's been brainwashed by the commercialism forces ruling less like kings and more like dark phantoms over her life, we still don't really know her, right? So we don't say anything we can't take back, reminding ourselves how right we felt just moments before when we realized we were in an anti-TV/pro-radio zone. So we stare at the asshole. The asshole stares at us. And eventually the asshole waltzes back into the studio to change out the controversial track that's about to time out and the matter is dropped entirely.

*

One summer I get asked out by three eligible guys in a row. I believe my time has finally come. I am desirable! It's not your hair, says Keely. Or your personality. It's the pheromones you're unleashing. I am appalled that she has taken my identity out of the equation. But before I have a chance to tell her she has offended me, I realize none of the three guys who have asked me out are eligible after all—they are just assholes who have somehow gotten the impression that I'm an easy lay.

*

When we file the records back in the stacks, we are sure to file the records quietly. When we tip-toe down the hallway in our sock-feet to use the bathroom during an extended track, we are sure to tip-toe quietly. When we answer the ringing phone late at night, we are sure to address the caller quietly. Hello? we are apt to say. Why are we whispering? the caller is apt to say back. When we think we hear the ghost capering through the studio, we are sure to listen in as if a doctor to a heart, quietly. The Librarian says the ghost will only waft through the studio when you're oblivious that he's there. And if anyone knows the tendencies of ghost in the studio it's the Librarian, right? We have no reason not to believe the ghost in the studio is real. Yet even in our humble and wholehearted belief, we can never understand why the ghost in the studio only ever makes noise that is quieter than the noise we make.

*

Do you drink heavily? Tolerate smoked substances? Overcooked omelets? Roommate obligations that may or may not include hair styling, vomit whitewashing, drilling new holes for screws unleashed during late night activity? Have you ever been victim to a chemical burn? Can your stomach tolerate expired foods such as moldy bread, sour milk, limp celery? Can you add to our sizable record collection or merely duplicate it? Do you own noise-cancellation headgear or know where to acquire such equipment at little to no cost? In four sentences or fewer, describe your quest to revitalize the post-punk movement. In three sentences or fewer, state your reasons for denouncing Bright Eyes, Ani DiFranco, new metal, smooth jazz and Sunday school. In two sentences or fewer, bequeath your autographed and rare vinyl LPs to us upon your accidental death and the room is yours.

*

When the freegans wander off with our recycled paper bin again, the campus police knock on the station's office. We are aghast to learn that our bank statements line the backs of show flyers that were illegally stapled to telephone poles around town. Do we know who the culprits are? Deep down I have the conviction to tell the campus police the truth. But the freegans barely have first names, let alone last names, so what information do we really have to give? Then my palms begin to sweat because I remember the pot in the small pouch of my backpack. But do the police even know my full name? It's in this moment that I realize how analogous I am to the freegans after all. I vow never to turn them in. To this day I feel immense pride for this minuscule promise I have kept.

*

All semester long I answer hoping that the caller is the Day Art deejay who I like. For my last show I play the bands he also likes, thinking I am sending him a super secret message across the airwaves. When I'm down to the final minutes I get on the mic and say, This last song is for a mystery secret person who shalt not be named. I am pleased with the mystery I have conspired and wait for the last time for the phone to ring. When it does, I answer emphatically, hopefully, Yes? but am not surprised even then that the caller is the next deejay's girlfriend. Can I pass a message along? Yes, I can pass a message along. Phish is reuniting, she says. They're touring again! she says. I am frustrated, only I am uncertain whether my frustration is because I have not heard from the Day Art deejay who I like or because of the enthusiasm in the caller's voice. When the next deejay fails to arrive promptly, I cue the mic again, selfishly hoping to spoil the surprise. Phish is reuniting, I say, only I disguise my voice when I say this to mimic the automated Radiobot. Then I turn on the automated Radiobot as per the instructions of what to do when no deejay is present and walk out. As I walk home my frustration lessens. Despite the now certain knowledge that the Day Art deejay who I like does in no way like me, I can only be pleased that, in one sense, I have fulfilled my final caller's request.

*

Is nonstop indie pop a completely terrible idea for a show? Nonstop indie pop is not a completely terrible idea for a show. Is nonstop indie pop a mostly terrible idea for show? It's not impossible that nonstop indie pop is a mostly terrible idea for a show. Will we grant them the timeslot they want to air their possibly mostly terrible idea for a nonstop indie pop show? We will review the applications for other ideas for a show before we grant anyone with any ideas a show. After review of the applications for other ideas for a show and in conclusion: we indeed will grant them the timeslot they want to air their possibly mostly terrible idea for a show.

*

In the old song that we love she is suffering for a boy but in real life when we see her in the bathroom before her set she is calm and confident and puts on her lipstick without turning her mouth down or up. The lyrics to her new songs go shake it, shake it, shake or they go you can be in on the take but we are not so sure these are the lyrics we've come to expect from her. Didn't she just sing about heartbreak and shattering and woe? Wasn't her last album so dark and full of pain? When she sings the new songs we are sure that we still love her—for all the fodder she has given us there is no giving back—but we are terribly perplexed about what transpired in her life that would mend her heartache so soon.

*

When the impossible happens and we tire of browsing the thousands upon thousands of records in the stacks and we have drank all the beer, we air the entire B-side of White Light/White Heat and play the game of "what's probably going to happen to us." The News Director says it's likely we will never have real jobs anyway so none of us will ever own a house that our parents don't buy us. The Promotions Director says we're probably all going to have more than our fair share of unprotected sex out of wedlock without ever really considering the consequences. The Junior Sales Manager says we will keep forming bands that have no fans and play countless shows for invisible audiences. I am not unsure we won't have hereditary diseases. Contracted diseases, the Promotions Director says. He says, You mean diseases we didn't think we'd ever get. Before I can tell him he misunderstands me—I mean hereditary diseases that we don't know we have—the record ends and we have to muster our collective energy once again to step outside ourselves and our invented problems and instead address our reality, the one we sometimes forget is to please or not please—or at the very least project upon—our increasingly marginal listening audience.

*

For fear of being ostracized by our classmates, we refrain from wearing our "Funnest Radio Station in the World" T-shirts to our literature classes. During an in-class recitation of "The Waste Land," we vow to print new T-shirts. We use the time in class to dabble in the design of a new T-shirt. We sketch a robot with a boombox for a brain. We sketch a brain with headphones for ears. We sketch a boombox squaring off with a pair of headphones with a brain looking on. After class we discuss collectively signing up for a graphic design class and make a combined mental note to look up the classes offered next semester. During two more classes of in-class poetry recitations, we sketch out a handful of other ideas, none of which seem immediately terrible. Days later we are all strongly considering a major in graphic design instead of literature. Days later still, we think, whether rightly or wrongly, that the solutions to our lifetimes of crippling embarrassments may be different than we originally thought.

*

The barefoot hippie does not have a radio show but hovers around the station when deejays he knows are on-air. The barefoot hippie walks barefoot to all the bars and all the parties and on all the grassy knolls and campus lawns. The barefoot hippie does not have a good diet but he tells us it is because he is intolerant of most foods. The digestive system is rough, OK? Mostly the barefoot hippie is kind though sometimes he is in a mood and says an unkind kind of thing. Sometimes we take offense and sometimes we disregard his unkindness as a ruse. There's no reason to overreact to the barefoot hippie, right? Sometimes we offer to buy him a drink that he can tolerate and sit with him and chat, as we are doing tonight, as we have done before. Sometimes we think the barefoot hippie is odd, odd, odd, but never do we think he will do the ghastly things he eventually does. Never do we think he will be a convicted murderer on death row. Never do we wonder this as he is telling us a story of foraging in the woods, as we laugh at his quirks, as we enjoy the night air and the party and the stoop. Never in any light do we see that this man, this man who in this moment may only lack a good pair of shoes and a laxative, is capable of very certain things that we are not.

*

The drummer and bass player are staying at Fun Pauly's and the lead guitarist is sleeping in the van because when you're born in the woods you can pass out just about anywhere comfortably. But where will the other guitarist sleep? I can only hope that when the Day Art deejay sees me leaving with the other guitarist, jealousy might rise up in him like lava heaves up a volcano. When the show ends I stand near the entryway to the house to enact my plan, thinking that the other guitarist will come out any moment and say, OK, you ready? And off we'll go, passing the Day Art deejay who I like just in time for him to see what's unfolding in my life. But it's getting late and the show's breaking up and the Day Art deejay is making his rounds of goodbyes and still the other guitarist hasn't emerged from the house. When he finally does, I'm sitting alone on the ground, practically dirt in hand, and when I wave to him in effort not to look upset he says, Sorry, but what's your name again? You're Keely, right? Despite the devastation I feel and the failure that I now know lurks in every cranny of my life, I don't correct him immediately. I only say, This way, come on, it's really a pleasant walk. I say, Maybe if we're lucky Keely will beat us there.

*

The question we want to know is a basic question: What kind of irresponsible person applies for a coveted summer show, only to sleep through it two weeks in a row? Even more basic is: Where the fuck were you, Kevin? Kevin does not immediately vocalize a response, only throws up his hands in the air and huffs and huffs as if he's a whale winding down. Finally we hear him say something to the effect of, I've been on time for every show three semesters straight and this is how you repay me? Oh ye of never slacking off! Later that summer when I am too hung over and tired to get out of bed to make it in time to cover the slot vacant after Kevin's firing, I break into sobs. I fail to fall asleep again. My head rings, vibrates, then rings louder. I cry intermittently throughout the morning, realizing with extreme certainty that it's only a matter of time before I will have to get a paying job, one that will surely not tolerate such carelessness.

*

Although Sara's social stakes are low in this town, Sara is clearly nervous to be a guest on my show. I announce to the listening audience that two years ago my best friend Sara went away to college in a different state. Today she is visiting and is a guest on my show. I say, Hi, Sara! and signal her to speak. When she shakes her head and waves her hands in manner to indicate, Noooo, I'm not talking on-air! I laugh nervously. I say, It seems Sara is a bit shy. I say, Maybe we'll try her again later. When the show is almost over, I slyly cue up the mics again and try to catch Sara off-guard. What did you think of the show, Sara? When she still refuses to respond, I get desperate. Wasn't it Put-a-Sock-in-it Sara they used to call you in high school? Wasn't it you who could never shut up? The accusations garner a fit of guffaws and sounds of audible denial. I could not have planned it better. Dramatically Sara storms down the hallway to the bathroom, but I am not distraught. Rather, I am at ease in giving the listening audience evidence that Sara was indeed in town visiting, thereby dispelling any notions that I am unable to maintain the complexities of a steady and close friendship.

*

Because my lover is a bartender at the busiest bar downtown I drink underage at many of the bars downtown. Finally I am legal and am so smitten that I bar-crawl from one bar of former trespass to the next. At the third bar I am already so drunk I begin telling everyone that today, today I am 21! I hope they will pour me free shots as they are want to pour others who turn the legal age but my announcement is met with outrage and protest. What do you mean today, huh? Haven't you been drinking here for like two whole years? Don't you get drunk here every weekend? You could've gotten us in some serious trouble! Their outrage makes me feel like the criminal that I am, and I sit for some time at the bar in silence, deliriously rejected. But when the kitchen manager comes over to applaud my escapades and in the midst of the applause asks if he can take me out sometime, my outlook changes. In my now legal drunkenness I feel like a mastermind—a real hero for the times!—for it is I who has gotten away with the most socially-gratifying crime of all.

*

Keely and I meet for lunch in the student commons when we are both between classes. What else are we both between? I mull over possible answers in my mind: boyfriends, trips home to see our parents, fits of drunken rages. Before I voice any answers, Keely says she has great news. I'm dating someone, she says. She says, Someone you know too. I am unsure whether to guess names of people we both know or wait until she tells me who it is. I chew my salad in a way to suggest that the chewing is preventing me from talking. I try to stretch the chewing for as long as possible before swallowing. I imagine in those moments of chewing that this same conversation is happening in another dimension, only in another dimension I'm the one announcing the great news of my new boyfriend to Keely. Finally Keely says, Well, don't you want to know who he is? Realizing then that I have been the worst possible friend in this moment, I emit a possibly exaggerated response to overcompensate. Yes! Yes! Who is it? When she doesn't name the Day Art deejay, I am immediately relieved. Wow, I say. Wow. That's great, I say, adding, I thought for a minute you might be dating Ben Kingsly. Oh, no, Keely says. Him? I could never seriously date a guy who was lousy in the sack. I laugh nervously, and in that moment realize something else about myself that seems to outweigh my prior realization of being a poor friend: I will always and forever lack the courage to ask how she knows this most interesting fact.

*

The Saturn Haus is around the corner but it takes two years and a winter's dark for me to finally show. I stand in the kitchen drinking a PBR. I stand in the hallway drinking a PBR. I take the stairs to the second floor and pretend to take intermittent sips of what was previously a can full of PBR. There are more PBRs in the corner but they're tied up like dogs to a sled. The second band is louder than the first band. Is the second band better than the first band? It's not improbable that the bass player looks in my direction more than a handful of times. Despite my uneasiness, I catch myself smiling throughout the night, though I'm unsure who I am smiling at. The crowd is louder than the third band. Give that band more mic! What we cannot know is that the windows will give as the band taunts the crowd and the crowd will go flying through and land on the brick patio below. What we cannot further know is that later that night we will all be detained by the police and interviewed against a backdrop of wails. The person who died is not someone I know. When it's my turn to be interviewed, I am too stunned to tell if I am crying or not crying. I am too stunned to remember whether I tell the police I know everyone there or that I know no one. I either tell them something or nothing they don't already know. I walk home alone, unsure if know anything anymore at all.

*

In efforts to make the mandatory organizational meeting seem less dull, we call the meeting our Semi-annual Orgy. We post graphic images announcing the mandatory orgy to all deejays. To recruit new deejay apprentices, we stand outside the student commons and pass out lewd flyers to the Year's Best Orgy. To combat our nervousness, we down countless shots of whiskey on the day of the meeting before standing in front of the large crowd that has gathered. We introduce ourselves as if we're part of a production company that films pornos. We pass around a sign-in sheet for current deejays and a sign-up sheet for new blood. Only after the meeting when a busty girl comes forward to show us her cleavage tattoos and nipple piercings do we realize that our joke has gone too far. The Program Director quits on the spot, citing that he doesn't have any real potential apprentices for the AM frequency and therefore will fail at his recruitment responsibilities. Years later when I am walking home late at night in a robust city district, I am handed a flyer to what appears to be an actual orgy. I am reminded that years earlier I was too drunk at the fake orgy to care about everything that went wrong.

*

The thunderstorm breaks just as we say the station identification that leads into the second hour of the Night Art we are subbing. We crack the windows in the studio to amplify the sounds of the rain. We choose tracks from then on out that sound like the kind of tracks you'd want to listen to during a thunderstorm. The callers are pleased with our selections. How about some more Mogwai? they ask. Explosions in the Sky? Can? Tel Aviv? Yes, we say, all good bands to accompany the rain! More, more rain! we say. When sadly the show that feels less like a chore and more like a fate that's crossed us comes to an end, we pack our things and take the stairs to the street level. Still, there is rain. Oh, the glorious rain! we say. And we keep this feeling close to us until the inevitable frustration rolls in, as we dig through our bags to find that neither of us had the foresight to bring an umbrella and or rain repellent of any kind. For the next hour we stand under the awning and listen to the rain, now void of its musical accompaniment, feeling surely as if the gods are punishing us for the overstated joy we so recently and shortsightedly felt.

*

The one Keely wants has a sun porch, a dishwasher, ceiling fans in every room and allows small dogs. The one I want has individual rooms off a halfway and a community bathroom and is two flights above the cellar bar. We do rock, paper, scissors, but when Keely wins I say, But you know I'm allergic to dogs, right? So we do rock, paper, scissors again and when Keely wins again she doesn't say, Best out of five? only sighs so loudly you think the ghost in the station will spook. So it's us packing our boxes separately and getting a moving van separately and moving into our new apartments separately. And when in the new apartment I'm hanging the photograph I have of me and Keely to hang, my brain almost tries to hang it separately. And when years later I move into yet another apartment, my brain doesn't even separate itself so my hands can hang the photograph. And when I move into yet another apartment in a different city many, many years later, I search everywhere for the photograph because there's a perfect spot in the hallway for it to hang. Only then do I realize the photograph has been lost over the series of moves.

*

Are we jealous of the deejay whose Night Art show happens to fall on Halloween? Yes, we are jealous of the deejay whose Night Art show happens to fall on Halloween. Does someone on staff throw a party for us to dance drunkenly to the Night Art show playing on Halloween? Yes, someone on staff throws a party for us to dance drunkenly to the Night Art show playing on Halloween. Do we wear hodgepodge and indecent homemade costumes to the drunken Night Art Halloween dance party? Yes, the festive among us wear hodgepodge and indecent homemade costumes to the drunken Night Art Halloween dance party. But do we wait at the end of the night for the Halloween Night Art deejay to arrive and celebrate with us? Do we even think to invite the Halloween Night Art deejay over? This is the downside to being the deejay whose Night Art show happens to fall on Halloween.

*

The Official List of Records Missing is posted on the wall of Official Office Posts Only. The Official List of Records Missing include: The Cramps' Psychedelic Jungle, Meat Beat Manifesto's RUOK?, Jonathan Richman's I, Jonathan, God is My Co-Pilot's I am not this Body, every Lords of Acid album of the '90s. On first glance, there appears to be over 100 records on the Official List of Records Missing. Under closer scrutiny, it appears that many of the entries on the Official List of Records Missing have been entered twice: once by the Librarian, who is the person officially responsible for maintaining the Official List of Records Missing, and once by a deejay who noticed a record missing and decided to handwrite it onto the list before checking if it was already listed on the Official List of Records Missing. Also, some of the records on the Official List of Records Missing have been crossed out, meaning they have been found or returned to their designated shelf space in the music library or have been deemed too irrelevant of our efforts to find them. Whenever browsing the Official List of Records Missing, a series of questions emerge: What do these records have in common? Do the lyrics of the records perhaps inspire aversion to authority? Do the artists maintain similar stances on abortion, gun control, legalization of marijuana? Did any of the records glean similarly bad or similarly good reviews upon release? Did the cover art offend people? Despite the inaccuracy with which we answer most of the questions, we feel rewarded for the progress we make towards discovering the culprits behind the records missing. Whether rightly or wrongly, more than once we have looked at each other and thought: we should've been detectives.

*

From the studio comes fits of laughter. Heaving guffaws and on-air flirtations. Plenty of heavy panting. Is that popcorn I smell? Hot roasted nuts? Empty beer bottles line the hallway. Remnants from some sort of a drinking game. Or a line up to keep count? Then one fired-up tobacco masking the stench of something enviable. Garments can be hard to identify when flying fearlessly through the air. Are those boxers or briefs? Moans of pleasure or annoyance? Clearly I cannot stay crouched in this position much longer.

*

In the dream, the Day Art deejay had the look of going. I said, Are you staying or going? Turned to cue up the next track and thought he was already gone. He'd only gone down the hall to take a leak. He now had the look of staying. Just like old times, he picked the next track. Then I picked the one after that. And he picked the one after that. You get the idea. Piggyback radio, he called it. Leapfrog radio, I said. Not like either of us was more correct. The Day Art deejay walked me home after the show. We stood at my front door that led onto the second floor landing above the cellar bar. Again he had the look of going. Stay, I said. He did. Once again he disappeared down the hall to take a leak. For as long as I'd known him, he was always taking leaks down a hall. Why would this time be any different? I must've had the look of unknowing. The one of what next. We could take turns picking a record, he said. He said, Jumping Jehoshaphat Records! I said, Records Roulette! Neither of us had ever really cared what we called it. It's been a decade or more since I've seen the Day Art deejay, yet even as I wake from this most impossible dream I know that it is still possible that over a span of ten years he dreamed more or less favorably of me once too.

*

In class we learn that we are a captive audience and walk back to the radio station dismayed. Is it that we'd thought all our choices were ours all along? Is it that we never considered the influence of the capitalist machine? It is all we can do now but play a series of obscure and unpopular records louder than we've ever played them before, knowing all the while we eventually will have to stop playing the obscure and unpopular records and return to class, where we will now knowingly enter the tired cycle of captivity and sway and woe. And then: what?

*

More than once, someone who's clearly attuned to the transition of moods calls to say how much they are enjoying the show. They appreciate the journey from angry to sad to hopeful to fun-loving to melancholic. More than once, we're elated—the listeners can name all the moods! Also more than once, someone who's clearly not attuned to the transition of moods calls in a request. Can you play some Joy Division? someone asks. Got any Archers of Loaf in those stacks? New York Dolls? Gang of Four? What they cannot know is the devastation we feel when we obligingly put on their request. What they cannot know is that they are a buzz kill to the transition of moods. We want to please our listeners in the hope that they continue calling us and listening. But more than pleasing them and taking their calls and feeling the heartwarming feeling that is knowing they are listening, what we really want is for them to listen closer. What we really want is for them to recognize, once and for all, their most undeserved special selfish power to ruin the ebb and flow of everything.

*

My uncle calls in a new request every hour. Can you play some Talking Heads? John Prine? Crosby, Stills, & Nash? I can, I say, even though my cousins are always in the background bashing the piano keys and singing "Frosty the Snowman" or "Rudolph the Red-nosed Reindeer" when he calls. So how is that they're listening to me on the radio at the same time? Mema finally gets on the line and scolds me for not wearing a scarf to the station. You'll catch a cold, she says. You'll infect your lungs, she says. I tell her it's not as cold here as it is there. Hmph, she says. She says, It's not Thanksgiving without the whole family here and you know it.

*

The News Director is so talented and full of news and it is not long before he is offered a paying job at a radio station known for its continuous and thorough news. We are elated for him and his good fortune but also we are selfish and distraught. What will we do now that our good friend and colleague is gone? Who will be there to tell us what is important and what is news and what is not? How ever will we go on in a world of such unsubstantiated and imbalanced and imperfect news? In our grief we can only think of ourselves, until one day after a staff meeting we are righted. As we walk slowly and dejectedly downtown, it's the Junior Sales Manager who admits that the News Director is smart to get out. Hasn't radio always been a dying art? he says. The thought comforts us so greatly in the moment that we overcome our selfish thoughts and spend the rest of the night cheering and saluting the News Director's success. But years later when I have left radio behind to write poetry and novels instead, I take no comfort when I am told that literature is dying too.

*

The wedding may be fake, but the live deejay and strobe lights indicate that the dance party afterwards is quite real. Marty, the fake groom, yells over the music to ask if I want to dance. I nod but when I turn to put down my beer, he waltzes away with his fake bride Cynthia. I lean against the bar wondering if I should pick my beer back up. I scan the dancefloor to see if there's anyone else here that I know. The moment Keely arrives I yell over the music to tell her I am leaving, but because she cannot understand me I do not immediately go. Keely orders us a round of shots. Then another. Then two more. After we have long danced in the most drunken and ridiculous and shameless ways I finally feel desirable again. In the heat of my allure, I convince myself that I must have heard the fake groom wrong. And full of fake congratulations for all those around me, I decide to blame the strobe light for the initial mistake.

*

Are we qualified to demonstrate what punk rock and jazz have in common? After many years dabbling in both genres, we believe we are qualified to demonstrate what punk rock and jazz have in common. Can we put together a Radiothon theme called "Jazz…or Astrojazz?" that eloquently shows what punk rock and jazz have in common? We can put together a Radiothon theme called "Jazz...or Astrojazz?" that more or less eloquently shows what punk rock and jazz have in common. But can we get anyone other than our parents and roommates to donate to our Radiothon show? Can we do something to combat the station's slacking revenue in a downsized economy? As another week's worth of themed shows comes to an end, we are downtrodden to admit that we are not qualified to attempt such an objective and altruistic feat.

*

When we have run out plausible guesses, we pile into the News Director's car. When we get to the station, the door is locked. When we enter the studio, the airwaves are silent. No deejay is presently there, nor are there signs of one being there previously. We comb the stacks. Look under the console as the parent might spy under the bed or as the uninhibited among us might peer into the cookie jar. We can only walk out, shaking our heads in disbelief. We can only drive back to the party more spooked now than high, asking ourselves, Have you ever felt that a record fell into your hands as if to play itself on-air? Have you ever felt that the ghost was disappointed in your musical taste?

*

Accustomed to hearing certain music at a certain time of day, I tune in to the deejay who has taken over my timeslot. After he plays three tracks in a row that I don't recognize, I call in a request. But the deejay doesn't recognize the band I name. What's more, he says, he cannot locate the band in the stacks. I ask him if the Official List of Records Missing is still posted on the wall of Official Office Posts Only. I say, Perhaps the band I requested is on that list? Now I fear he might recognize who is on the phone, as if in citing the Official List of Records Missing I have given myself away. But all he says is, Why would the band you requested be on that list? He says, Are you saying that you stole the very record you requested? Instinctively I hang up the phone, realizing that in doing so I am indicting myself for the very crime I now wish I had committed.

*

The day before our radio show we often agree on the first song we will play on our radio show. For reasons that are still unclear to us, rarely do we think about the last song we will play on our radio show. For this reason the last song we play on our radio show is not always the most fitting last song to play on our radio show. But after more than three years on-air, what we can say is that what the last song always is is surprising.

*

Years later, walking past me down the street in a city hundreds of miles away is a man in a "Funnest Radio Station in the World" T-shirt. Hey, nice shirt! I call out. Hey, thanks! the man says. And I try to think of the best thing to say next while he goes back to eating his snow cone and crosses the street.

*

Because I am nervous I arrive at my poetry professor's house before the designated time. I wait gingerly in her foyer while she prepares tea. At the designated time she eagerly gives me a tour of the entire house, including her bedroom, where she sleeps on the same kind of mattress that the astronauts sleep on in space. I am to sleep on the astronaut mattress every night after I've given her arthritis-stricken cat his medication and have brushed him thoroughly from head to tail. I am to read her poetry books in her study as if I was her and pet her arthritis-stricken cat in my lap as she would. I am to wake in her stead and walk around the house imagining that I am a writer and professor of poetry myself. I am to thank her for the opportunity to live another life, a life of care and creation, even if only for the short time that she is away. My poetry professor—such a generous soul! Years later, when I am less nervous but still unsure of myself, I ask my poetry professor if she will write me a recommendation to study poetry in a graduate program. Immediately she turns angry and appalled. Heavens, no! she says. Whatever would inspire you to do such a thing? she says. She says, Can't you see that not everyone is fit to be a poet?

*

The year after I graduate, I begin working at an art center in a nearby city. One day at work news comes that a gunman is loose on campus. I watch the news obsessively and am appalled to hear that 32 people are dead. Not everyone who the gunman shoots dies, however. Later I learn that the Chief Engineer was someone who was shot and survived. Later still I learn he will be interviewed by major media and appear on numerous talk shows to recount his traumatic experience. Later even than that I learn that he will receive free tuition for the rest of his life and be asked what the university can do to help ease the physical and psychological pain he suffered. The Chief Engineer will request that the radio station never be sold. He will request that the radio station always remain in the hands of students. To this day I am unsure if he ever received assurance that his request will be honored. To this day I live in constant fear that the memories I created will one day be erased by power and authority and greed—and that I will be powerless to stop what maybe isn't even inevitable.

*

I start hanging out with a boy who's not a deejay. An architect, no less! We spend nearly every weekend hiking the nearby trails, then drinking gin and tonics on his balcony that overlooks a parking lot that's never full. Soon we're cooking steak dinners together. But rarely do I stay over, and when I do, we never undress. On my birthday he buys me a dozen roses. I wonder if the romantic gesture somehow obligates me to sleep with him. The next day I wake with the conviction that in no way should I feel obligated, knowing it's now a moot point. But am I obligated to say that the sex last night was good? Thus begins my lifelong uneasiness regarding the etiquette of graceless sexual exchanges.

*

At least two weeks have come and gone so when my professor points to me and says, Ahh, Ms. Dove, so nice of you to join us again! I'm petrified. I'm beside myself. I wonder if in a class of thirty-five he really keeps us straight in his gradebook or if he has it out for me. And what if he has it out for me? What if my professor has chosen to make my life an extension of what is clearly his own personal eighteenth-century hell? So now that I'm technically a literature major instead of a communication major I figure I should start coming to class again and pay attention to what's happening to all those Lilliputians.

*

The deejay on-air is telling the true story of what really happened to him on the way to the station. The deejay says the true story of what really happened to him on the way to the station is so unbelievable he couldn't even make it up. The deejay says we, the listening audience, will never believe the true story of what really happened to him on the way to the station but the story of what really happened to him is in fact 100 per cent true. The deejay says he wouldn't even believe the story of what really happened to him unless, of course, it had happened to him. Only after the deejay finally tells the true story of what really happened to him on the way to the station do we agree that the true story of what really happened to him is in no way true. For the sake of all humanity, we at least hope not.

*

Two hours pass and the phone has yet to ring. No one has come into the office to see what mail has arrived or has stopped in to say they are enjoying the show. I cue up the next track I will play but let the current track playing time out and do not immediately drop the needle. I soak in the sound of dead air for longer than I should. I do not know if the silence is a cry for help or who it really is that I want to speak to or see. I do not know how to be any more naked before the indifferent world. It's in this moment before I finally play the song that is cued up to play that I feel what it feels to be utterly pointless. Yet immediately after the moment of pointlessness comes exhilaration, as I know now that the most vulnerable I have ever been has passed—and still I am me.

*

The music I play is angry and loud and discordant and affected, so why wouldn't I turn up the volume in the studio to an uncomfortable level? I go on this way for several tracks, not caring one mousey minutia about the disturbance I am issuing down the media hall. When I look up from my half-star of a head bang, the girl standing in the doorway looks disturbed. I thought you would've been a boy, she says. Oh, I say. This band is rad, she says. Tell me about it, I say. We say nothing more while the song continues to play over the airwaves. The next track is a band she does not know. She sits on the couch to listen as if she's a guest on my show. She sits and she listens and when the bridge comes I turn up the volume another notch and then another and she looks right at me and smiles.

*

The Program Director says the Day Art deejay who plays only vinyl from the Americana stacks is the epitome of cool. The News Director says the Night Art deejay who plays only 45s from the soul bins is the epitome of cool. The Chief Engineer says the new music deejay who plays only tracks off his computer is the exact opposite of cool—they are so ridiculous they are in fact uncool! I say nothing and wait until everyone at the table comes to the same revelation at which I have arrived. When we order a third round of drinks the revelation finally sinks in. That is, despite our disagreement as to what may or may not constitute a combination of cool, we should at the very least agree on one thing: discussions about who is the epitome of cool or who is uncool is one blatant act that makes us so very uncool.

*

We choose "Songs from the Future about the Past" and unwittingly try out some Radio Cacophony. The next year we choose "Songs from the Past about the Future" and make another failed attempt to layer songs on top of each other. When our shows yield the same low revenue year after year, we come to believe that the themes we choose ultimately do not influence donations. In a fluctuating economy, it is the stable audience who is our true downfall.

*

The record is winding down and I am out of records to play. I take a chance on a record I do not know and cue it without listening to it first. After four years on-air I should know by now that album artwork is not indicative of anything. Is this record a record that I like? Does it matter or not matter that the singer on the cover is obscured by a neon film? That his gaze into my eyes is foretelling of what angst and brooding is to come? When my concerns are thwarted I am relieved. I am left with the surprising sounds that arise only on a first listen—the sounds of exoticism and intrigue and, if I am as lucky as I am patient, belief.

*

A summer passes and a finely groomed boy from my modern poetry class wanders into the station. When he addresses me by name I panic. George? Garth? Gentry? Jim? My expression must expose my doubt. From last semester? he finally says. Remember? And his look of incredulity tells me that I ruined any chance at friendship of any sort. Weeks later I notice him standing across the street from me and I wave. Did I think he would wave back? I stay vigil many nights afterwards until I know my current classmates' names as if members of my extended family tree.

*

Soon after we graduate, Keely marries the Day Art deejay and moves to a northern state. Years pass. When she visits the city where I live for a conference, I instinctively begin where we left off. I name the bands I currently listen to, the bands I just saw, and the bands I have tickets to see in the future. I want to ask if the sex is better. But as a now college graduate I feel mature enough to refrain from posing questions I cannot reciprocate a reply to nor have the capacity to illustrate with personal examples.

*

Despite my aversion to camping, I have always wanted to go to bed with a dread-head. But his dreads are so heavy that I cannot fall asleep. I lay there for a small eternity, hoping maybe he will roll over or eventually need to take a leak. Yet he moves hardly an inch in his sleep. Finally I am delirious enough with sleep that I convince myself his dreads aren't lice-ridden tentacles at all, but giant cinnamon and sugar churros that I will eat in my dreams without gaining a single pound. Empty calories! The thought gives me enough pleasure to distract my neuroses and I fall asleep. But hours later I am awake again, realizing it's impossible to convince myself his snore is anything other than a monstrous beast, my body its conduit to intercede with the night.

*

When I answer the studio phone, I am surprised to discover I am known as the redhead who always wears blue. Irrespective of truth, I vow to counter this two-dimensional identity. I carry a neon green satchel when I go out to the bars. I wrap a Band-Aid around my finger even when nothing has stung me. I borrow a pair of my roommate's patchwork pants and don them at house parties. I pile my hair so high on my head it spills into a halo. I wear so many bangles to class the professor cannot ignore my raised hand. Years later I ask my friends what I am known for, and are they in agreement? My plan has worked! But when one of them says I am the only redhead he knows who likes Solex and Hot Snakes, I am mortified. Only I am unsure whether I am more upset that my hair is my true singularity or that I didn't just dye it in the first place.

*

I graduate from college but I do not immediately give up my prime radio slot. For haven't I worked so tirelessly only to have these two precious hours a week to show for it? Aren't these two hours what I have earned? I host my show into the next semester, until finally summer comes and I am ready to admit that I own nothing—not a thing in this world is truly mine—and I relinquish the cherished slot. In years following I half-heartedly attempt to work at many different community radio stations in many different cities. And when I am the closest I have ever been—when I am offered a training session at a progressive and influential community station—I disbelieve my ability to return to radio after all. Yet I excuse myself with a new delusion, declaring myself too beholden to writing to take on anything else of meaning or substance. Warily, I want the lie to be true.

*

When other prominent universities begin selling off their student radio frequencies left and right, we fear we're next. We launch a campaign to petition the rights to our frequency, thinking ourselves proactive. It works! Our campaign garners the university's attention and we're slated to speak before the Board of Visitors. The Provost asks to meet with us before we petition the board, claiming he'd like to coach us to empower our delivery. We are so nervous we readily agree. But when the Provost hears our full argument, he changes his mind. It'll never work, he says, and he cancels our appearance. It's only after we recover from feeling sheepish and dejected that we agree that it is the Provost who is truly proactive.

*

Keely is sitting in a back booth talking to the Day Art deejay. The Day Art deejay is waving across the bar to the Librarian. The Librarian is walking towards the Promotions Director. Is the Promotions Director sharing a pitcher and tater tots with the News Director? The News Director is talking so loudly I can hear him from where I'm sitting alone at the bar, waiting for the unscrupulous bartender to notice me. When the unscrupulous bartender finally notices me I do not take my eyes off him until I pay for my beer. It feels as if no time has passed but when I turn around there is no one waving or walking or talking to anyone I know. There is no one left at the bar who I know. I know I could set my beer down and walk down block to find them. I know I could turn and talk to the people I don't know sitting on either side of me at the bar. But what I know even more is a distillation and resolve deep within. There is nothing more logical and noble to do now except learn how to drink out of loneliness.

*

When we play the band who is the droniest of drone, someone phones in to say while great, they know a band who's dronier. When we pay the band who is so somber we could cry, someone phones in to say to it's the middle of the day—why are we out to make people cry? When we announce that we're about to play a new band we meant to play last week but forgot to play and are eager to hear, someone calls in to say he dislikes when we talk too much, OK? When our listening audience isn't listening at all, only calling in to hear themselves complain, sometimes we let them have their way. Other times we crudely let the phone ring. We are trapped in all the rote things.

*

When we pause for an elongated moment, we agree that the world is changing. When we agree that the world is changing, we discover that we feel faceless and unrecognized and consent the time has come to designate a proper mascot. But where to find such a three-dimensional cultured beast worthy of the role? We search the frat apartment dumpsters. The abandoned buildings and alleyways downtown. We call out Radio Cat, Radio Cat, here, here, Radio Cat into the night. Finally we make a PSA, though never does anyone call with any leads of Radio Cat's whereabouts. Even as we settle on a vaguely artful sketch of Van Boombox Man as our mascot instead, we remain convinced that Radio Cat is out there, roaming the night, as fearful of the ghosts as we too are forever afraid.

*

When the band is halfway through their set, I admit to my lover my lustful attraction to the drummer. I cup my hand around my lover's ear and list the lustful things I want to do to the drummer's body. My progressive and free lover—he encourages my sexuality! When the band finishes their set, I do not even notice my lover whispering something in the drummer's ear. But isn't it the only explanation as to why the drummer approaches me later in the evening and smiles so perversely? What am I doing later tonight, the drummer wants to know. He is even free tomorrow, he says, and he casually tucks his long, dark brown hair that is full of sheen behind his ear. My lover is nowhere in sight but I suspect he is somewhere nearby, watching the loaded exchange. I have no way of knowing what he has told the drummer, no way of knowing the extent of my imaginative trespass. The drummer holds his eyes on me as I search for the right reply. For nearly a full minute I am riddled and mute, until finally I blurt out the best lie I can muster. I can see in the drummer's reaction that he does not believe me. But I know now that he also does not believe what anyone has told him all night. More than that, I know now that it is doubt, not lust, that is the more resounding emotion.

*

The deejay wants to remain anonymous but because she wants to remain anonymous and we do not understand her want we decide to ridicule her instead. We name her Val M. and vow never to reveal that this is not her true identity. Over the course of the semester, we become so earnest in our wanting to sustain her false identity that we eventually forget she is not actually who we pretend her to be. And when the next semester comes around we do not even think twice before publishing her name as Val M. in the schedule. Riding the elevator with her to the studio one day, we are so high that we cannot stop giggling. But then all at once we are silenced. My name's not Val M., she says. It's Mary. Mary Bennington. Either we are too high or ashamed in the moment to vocalize an apology. It is then Mary who exits the elevator first, her posture the thing most informing us that we are the ones who are very in the wrong. In the office we reenact the exchange and become so uneasy that we decide to compose a formal apology. The apology is sincere, but when we get to the signature we are still unable to reign in our highness or our unkindness and do instead what we feel we must and sign the letter Four Anonymous Fans. As we sign the words we in one way feel relief and in another way know that we are asking for it. We know that we are masochists, and specific masochists at that, the very masochists who are granting the universe a retaliation much grander than any earthly ridicule we can enact, let alone conceive.

*

Because I don't have a summer job or any real responsibilities I get so terribly stoned with my friends and spread my body across the downtown lawn whenever I wish. I am as free as the ocean! But when my former literature professor approaches me from across the lawn I become trapped in my own mind. How's your summer, he asks. Have you been reading anything new and good, he wants to know. I am too high and vulnerable to give any acceptable response. In a moment too sudden to process, it is evident my former professor discovers my state of mind and becomes embarrassed for us both and hurriedly excuses himself. Could it have been my perverse silence that alerted him? Did my inability to stop smiling tell him something was up? Was it the spontaneous twirling that gave me away? To this day I remain mortified of the exchange, yet rest assured that I acted so effusively and complexly bizarre that neither of us will ever deduce what truly happened.

*

The theme we pick is "The Name Game," meaning we will only play songs with someone's name in them. We think we can encourage listeners to call in and tell us songs with his or her name in them because almost everyone knows a handful of songs with his or her name in them. This way we won't run out of songs to play. But knowing we won't run out of songs to play only makes us more nervous, since now we must focus on what truly matters—donations. And deep down we know that it is money that makes us the most nervous of all.

*

Despite years of controversial on-air personalities and nonpareil Radiothon themes, the station is running a deficit. We brainstorm new revenue streams. We solicit the advice of the News Director's father, a legitimate financial advisor. We launch new public relations campaigns. When the deficit increases we get unusually desperate. We try everything, but nothing gains any traction. When we finally think we're out of ideas, the Promotions Director initiates an impromptu Mustache-a-thon, announcing on-air that we refuse to shave until our donations match our shortfall. The most notorious deejays get on board. In less than two days' time, we have a solid movement. We have hope! We keep up the Mustache-a-thon for weeks, seeing a dollar here, dollar there. We want to believe that it's working, even when we know, in fact, it is not. After four disorienting weeks we call off the campaign. The Promotions Director is the last to become disheartened but the first to admit his fatal error: you can't see mustaches on the radio, can you? It's true, we all agree. And whether to ease the Promotion Director's heartbreak or to whitewash our own stupidity, nobody pretends that they'd known this all along.

*

With the start of the semester comes a string of good luck. I find a quarter on my way to the station. I am handed a punch card for a free fountain soda every time I buy a premium sandwich. I run into a friend of my mother who gives me the number of her handsome and now single son, along with her blessing to call him. I sit down at the console hoping my good luck will carry me through my first radio show in months. I happily field the listening audience's requests, confidently transitioning from one unexpected track to the next. When everything goes off smoothly, I become nervous in thinking something terrible is about to happen. I walk home with trepidation about where to step. I walk faster. I whistle vigorously. I look over one shoulder, then the other. I cannot shake the feeling that some evil is lurking in the night. I crawl into bed and pull the covers over my head. I have the worst sleep I've had in weeks, waking in fits during the night and wondering if I left the stove on or the door unlocked. I live in fear of inevitable doom for weeks, until finally something terrible happens. In the grocery store parking lot, I phone my neighbor. As I wait for him to bring the jumper cables, a thunderstorm breaks. I am so relieved that I begin sobbing. Despite my best efforts, I am in no condition to bear my string of good luck a moment longer.

*

Wading through the tattooed bodies and drunken cohorts does not give me nor Keely pause. Neither does the mosh pit that has naturally formed two feet in front of where we stand. Our only fear is mandated crowd participation, so imagine our relief when the band plays an encore without hesitation or whiff of applause. Walking home, Keely puts her head on my shoulder and asks me in the most serious way what I want out of life. She asks, You know, what matters to you? When no immediate answer comes to mind, I do not become distraught like I think I might. Instead I find myself developing less and less of an answer to her question, and only hoping more and more that bands will grant me the same autonomy at their shows as the band tonight granted me. I tell her, It is the realest of wants! Yet even in this moment of atypical clarity and want—with Keely's arm in my arm and the sky poured out like so much bathwater—I do not rejoice. I simply feel astute for accepting dissatisfaction at its core, unaware that years later I will look back and cringe for how little I understood of feminism, and how even less I knew of my privilege.

*

Now that I am the General Manager I am introduced by mutual friends to a former General Manager at the bar one night. The former General Manager is much taller than me and much older than me and much better at looking like he couldn't care less about anyone or anything and when I put my hand out to shake his hand he doesn't even acknowledge the gesture. This former General Manager and me—we have nothing in common.

*

The phone rings and because of the music I play on my radio show I am promptly invited to the mountain party. While I am unsure who else has been invited to the mountain party because of his or her radio show, I discretely ask around to find others, like me, who've been invited to the mountain party because of the music he or she plays on his or her radio show. When the night of the mountain party arrives, we pile into an invitee's car to drive the many miles to the mountain party. Yet when we arrive we are immediately confused. Around the fire pit are actual musicians, older men and women playing twelve-string guitars and lap guitars and banjos and tambourines and washboards and fiddles. Quickly we learn that the music they are playing at the mountain party is not the same as the music we play on our radio shows. Has there been some mistake? It takes nearly an hour but we eventually conclude that no, there has been no mistake. The mountain party isn't celebrating us, let alone the music we play. Rather the mountain party is an extension of the music sliver that we entertain in the world, showing us in the kindest way possible all it is that we can see and hear and be and do.

*

Years later I lie in bed at night trying to remember the name of someone from the radio station who I've forgotten. My failing memory brings frustration, but I am quick to remind myself that there's still hope. Because if I'd forgotten this person completely, would I even remember that I'd forgotten him? This is how I know I'm only half-gone, which is the eternal optimist's way to say still here. It's only when I visit the station many years later still that a greater worry sets in. Nothing is how I remember it. No band is shelved where I pulled it many years before from the stacks. The painted red wall is not even red. After the initial shock sets in, I return to my current city devoid of any familiar emotion. As weeks pass I become more and more suspect of myself. I spend countless hours trying to recall the slickest of childhood memories: the exhilaration and fear when pushed in the makeshift tire swing, the decision to quit horseback riding lessons when a classmate was trampled, the thorny sting of the rosebushes that wound up the front porch trellis. But even as I surface fleeting details of my childhood, can I ever be certain that I am accessing the memories I thought I forgot? Will I ever know if I cannot remember what it is I have truly forgotten? It is in this unknowing that I am humbled. It is entirely possible that over time I've abandoned not only the worst but the best memories of my life—and will never, not ever, get them back.

*

Preparing for the apocalypse, we find ourselves feverishly drunk and restless. The News Director asks how we're most afraid to go. The Promotions Director says by asteroid. The Junior Sales Manager says by solar radiation. Fun Pauly says he will not board a plane that's not flying over great bodies of water. When it's my turn I blurt out bear attack, although I know I'm lying. In truth I fear that I will choke on something that's been unsuspectingly lodged in my throat my lifelong. But I cannot admit the truth of what I direly fear in this moment, for what I fear even more is that such avid truth-telling will force the universe to pose a counterbalance. And then the apocalypse will really be upon us.

*

Although I could have recorded my radio show all along, I do not do so. When my last semester on-air is about to commence, I announce that I will record every show and mail the recordings the following year at random to fill the void when I am no longer on-air. But for all my excitement, I only remember my objective about halfway through every show. The semester passes and I fail to record anything but a few songs and an offensively voiced PSA. I fear that my friends will think me lazy or unreliable, yet no one ever says a derogatory thing or asks where their promised recording is. While I wish that I was the productive person I claimed to be, I more wish that I was the person who confronted my friends's false interest in my charitable endeavors.

*

I am almost to the door of the station—I am ten feet away!—when I realize I do not want to go in. That for all my goodwill and presence of mind, I cannot go in. I have been here countless times before, slept on the office couch through many classes, slept on the studio couch after many meals, taken many dosages of many kinds of drugs in the confines of the stacks. But what does home feel like anyway—and when do you know that where you are, which is where you have consistently been, is no longer it?

*

Years later I try to apply Radio Cacophony to the world. I layer the clothes I wear. I watch a movie while listening to a record while reciting a poem aloud. I turn on four appliances at once—blender, microwave, toaster oven, vacuum—and listen for the angelic hum that is their harmony. But when I try to do many tasks simultaneously at my desk job I am frustrated at how the disorder elongates my day. And when I invite many friends who do not know each other to the same bar I am disheartened when they talk over each other. What nonsense! It takes many more repeat offenses before I learn why I chose literature over mathematics in the first place: that is, even when the method is the same, it is our expectation for similar results that always lets us down.

*

We choose "Songs to Laugh Track By" and tell the punchlines of jokes in between songs. The punchlines we tell are mostly from jokes our dads retell at holiday dinners. When no one's called in to donate halfway through the show, it's evident our punchlines aren't funny on their own. Were we prepared for this? We were prepared for this, but we agree we are too far in to revamp the show. For more than we are prepared, we are stubborn.

*

I enter the studio and find myself face-to-face with the Day Art deejay. I have imagined this moment countless times before and delve into my imagination for what comes next. I conjure the time we rode unicorns down to the riverbed, the time we stole apples from an orchard off the highway, the time we made love on a rooftop in the river country. I fight the urge to tell him how much I've enjoyed our imagined time together, eventually blurting out how much I liked the last two tracks he aired before turning and walking out. It takes some effort, but I leave that day triumphant that I only said boring things.

*

There is only one tub of Jell-O but also only one stripper who wants to wrestle. And who among us non-strippers will wrestle her? Who will be so foolish to strip down to their bra and panties in the chilled fall night and step into the tub? Who will allow themselves to be most assuredly humiliated before the crowd that has gathered? Afterwards, when I shower with the stripper to remove the red Jell-O that has begun to seep into the depths of my skin and crevices of my body, I am so empowered that I do not mind how cold the water is. And later in the evening I get so drunk that I wake the next morning and forget temporarily how my undergarments became so stained and discolored. Later still, as I try to erase the red Jell-O from my most expensive bra to no avail while coughing and sneezing and wheezing uncontrollably, I become so certain that there indeed are seasons of growth—and equal acts of seasonal regret.

*

When the time has come for me to train the new General Manager, we meet in the station office to commence the training. We review the contents of the computer folders, the contents of the file cabinet, the contents of the drawers in the desk. In no time we are bored, so we walk to the bar to continue the training. On the way we stop to get our noses pierced—the tattoo parlor is running a special!—and when we get to the bar we sit in the back corner and try not to scratch our noses as we tell each other funny and embarrassing stories late into the night. The new General Manager is a riot! When I see the new General Manager the following week and ask how it's going, she is perplexed. She knows nothing about her role as General Manager. She doesn't remember what is in any of the folders or file cabinets. She is sure she will fail at her managerial responsibilities when the semester starts. As she tells me her worst fears of what will surely go wrong, she sips her beer with trepidation and unease. I am so taken with this new General Manager. She is more prepared than she knows.

*

Why do we love his eclectic radio show? If we could put a finger on why we love his eclectic radio show, we wouldn't shy away from him when he's sitting alone at the bar. If we could articulate what we truly love about his eclectic radio show, we'd pull up the barstool beside him and tell him everything he always wanted to hear. We'd confirm that what he was doing on his eclectic radio show was exactly what we, the listening audience, inferred that he was doing on his eclectic radio show. We'd tell him, You're doing it right! We get it! We do! We'd say, You were born to do your eclectic radio show! You're a natural! But even if we could verbalize why we love his eclectic radio show, could we ever be certain that our love is genuine? Could we ever know that our love for his eclectic radio show is a love that will last? Given the various format and genre changes that his eclectic radio show has undergone from year to year, the one thing we are sure of is that we cannot know our future feelings for certain.

*

There are the questions we could've been asking—what does music teach us about repetition? I mean, what does repetition teach us about heartbreak? I mean, what does heartbreak have in common with music? That is, what do compilations teach us about business? What do record labels teach us about division? What does broadcasting tell us about discipline? Who in god's name makes music without conviction? What kind of monstrosity lords over our personal taste and decisions? Why can't the music we love subsist without some kind of outside compensation? How many times will we forget our own participation? I mean, who doesn't have an undisclosed opinion? These are the questions that Twin A is not so sure that we weren't asking all along. Twin B, on the other hand, is confident we never asked them, will never ask them, are not even asking them now. That is, Twin B says, it's time to accept that we will never know the answers to the questions confounding us if we tried.

*

Many years later I decide I am ready to have children. Out of both propriety and compulsion, I ask the man I am with if he too is ready. He gives an affirmative reply and I am overjoyed. When months pass without any results, I become perplexed. I worry I am too anxious to host a fetus or, worse, infertile. In my self-absorbed state, I consider all the times in my life that I tried so desperately not to become pregnant. It takes some effort, but I manage to convince myself that I have not done irreversible psychological damage to my uterus. As in most things, I believe I simply must be let down before I can feel truly rewarded.

*

At the job interview, I wait for the moment when the interviewer asks about my time at the radio station. I answer all the questions leading up to the questions about the radio station. I wait for the interviewer to ask me how my experience at the radio station has prepared me for the open position. I shake his hand when I leave, hoping it's my chance to make small talk about the radio station. When no chance presents itself, I wait for the phone call about the job. I write him a follow-up email. I am prepared to answer any questions about how the radio station has shaped my life and professional trajectory. Years later, after no potential employer has ever asked about my experience at the radio station, I consider removing the radio station from my resume entirely. But deep down I believe there's still a chance it will one day matter. I cannot give up hope that the accumulation of an artful life will one day make sense.

*

Fearing that Alzheimer's is inevitable, I post a list of bands that I like next to the bathroom mirror. Every day I wake and review the list of bands that I like, adding names of new bands that I like whenever necessary. Effortlessly I come to memorize the list. Such self-actualizing cultural progress! Weeks pass and I add more and more names to the list of bands that I like. In a year's time I boast an impressive list of bands that I like. Congratulating myself, I soon stop adding to the list of bands that I like and the list of bands that I like remains a static thing that stares back at me every day. Over time I stop noticing the list altogether, having become so used to its presence and form unchanged, until one day I hear a band I do not know coming from my neighbor's house. The unnameable and pleasing sounds frustrate me, and in a panic I ball up the list of bands that I like and throw it away. I am disheartened to admit how even when I list all the bands that I like, I will never account for the bands that I like that I haven't yet heard, will never hear, let alone those who have yet to record a single note.

*

I worry the person on the radio is not me. And is the voice on the radio my voice? I employ the trick when I'm alone in the studio: kill the volume in the FM studio and broadcast the FM frequency from the AM studio across the hall. The effect is an echo as I talk, a personal ghost. Every time I cue the mic, I return to myself from another room. Is it the reassurance I seek? I only know that I do not recognize the voice billowing from the other room in full. There is still a chance that I am more myself every day.

*

Is anyone at the Ten Year Media Reunion someone who I expect to see? No one at the Ten Year Media Reunion is someone who I expect to see. Is anyone at the Ten Year Media Reunion someone who I desire but do not expect to see? There is one person at the Ten Year Media Reunion who I desire but do not expect to see. But does this person who I desire but do not expect to see desire to see me? Does this person even think to greet me with a hug, let alone part from me for another ten or more years with an embrace? It is for this reason that I drink too much at the Ten Year Media Reunion and sleep with a former features editor who was known for inverting correctly written sentences minutes before the newspaper went to press. And when the former features editor wakes early to dress and catch his train home I do not blush when he finds my bra in his jacket sleeve. But it takes all of my patience not to ask him if he had a good time at the party last night or if a good time last night at the party had he.

*

The Librarian buys us tickets to a show of the band we mutually love who's playing on my birthday. Five hours away we run into other deejays we know who say, Get out! We love this band too! We are so happy we are all together in a city five hours away seeing the band we mutually love that we down countless shots during the opening bands' sets to celebrate. When the band we mutually love appears on stage we cheer emphatically. When they play all our favorite songs we almost feel faint. When the show is over we cannot contain our bliss. Driving home, the Librarian asks what I liked most about the show of the band we mutually love. It is only then, upon sobering, that I realize I was too drunk at the show of the band we mutually love to truly focus on the band we mutually love. I fail to recall even two songs the band played. I spend the rest of the drive conflicted about the night. I want to blame my fellow deejays for my excessive and wasteful behavior, but deep down I know that I can only despise myself for altering the memory I thought I was supposed to make.

Acknowledgements

Many thanks to the editors of the publications where sections of this book appeared, sometimes in slightly different forms: *Chicago Review, Untoward, Pink Line Project,* and *Alice Blue Review.*

Thanks to WUVT-FM and the many individuals without whom this book would not exist: Josh Arritt, Len Comarrata, Mike MacKenzie, Evan MacKenzie, Neil Wettstein, Hilary Fussell Sisco, Dan Sisco, Daniel Owens, Bobby Cardoni, Michelle Belinkie, Thom Novario, Nathan Bowles, John Peters, Josh Seymour, Harvey Clark, Jack Bennett, Samantha Simmons Fredieu, Chris Jackson, Jeff Pineda, Dan Grubb, Aaron Horst, Sarah Jones Decker, Stephanie Sullivan, Ryan Vernon, Michael Castelhano, and Elliott Wrenn.

Thanks also to everyone who gave the book voice along the way to publication, especially Jenny Molberg, Meg Ronan, K. Lorraine Graham, Rod Smith, Buck Downs, Tracy Dimond, Tony Mancus, Amanda Petrusich, Kelly Schirmann, and Elisa Ambrogio.

Extended gratitude and infinite love to Mark Cugini and Laura Spencer and everyone at Big Lucks. Extra special thanks to Sally Anne Morgan for her wonderful cover design.

Also from Big Lucks Books

Chateau Wichman, Ben Pease

Fat Daisies, Carrie Murphy

The Good Life, Brandon Brown

Pink Museum, Caroline Crew

Wastoid, Mathias Svalina

Wildlives, Sarah Jean Alexander

Made in the USA
Lexington, KY
21 May 2017